# GULLIVER'S TRAVELS

JONATHAN SWIFT

SADDLEBACK
EDUCATIONAL PUBLISHING

# Saddleback's *Illustrated Classics*™

Three Watson
Irvine, CA 92618-2767
Website: www.sdlback.com

*ISBN-13: 978-1-56254-902-2*
*ISBN-10: 1-56254-902-2*
*eBook: 978-1-60291-150-5*

Printed in China

# Welcome to
# Saddleback's *Illustrated Classics*™

We are proud to welcome you to Saddleback's *Illustrated Classics*™. Saddleback's *Illustrated Classics*™ was designed specifically for the classroom to introduce readers to many of the great classics in literature. Each text, written and adapted by teachers and researchers, has been edited using the Dale-Chall vocabulary system. In addition, much time and effort has been spent to ensure that these high-interest stories retain all of the excitement, intrigue, and adventure of the original books.

With these graphically *Illustrated Classics*™, you learn what happens in the story in a number of different ways. One way is by reading the words a character says. Another way is by looking at the drawings of the character. The artist can tell you what kind of person a character is and what he or she is thinking or feeling.

This series will help you to develop confidence and a sense of accomplishment as you finish each novel. The stories in Saddleback's *Illustrated Classics*™ are fun to read. And remember, fun motivates!

# Overview

Everyone deserves to read the best literature our language has to offer. Saddleback's *Illustrated Classics*™ was designed to acquaint readers with the most famous stories from the world's greatest authors, while teaching essential skills. You will learn how to:

• Establish a purpose for reading
• Use prior knowledge
• Evaluate your reading
• Listen to the language as it is written
• Extend literary and language appreciation through discussion and
   writing activities

Reading is one of the most important skills you will ever learn. It provides the key to all kinds of information. By reading the *Illustrated Classics*™ , you will develop confidence and the self-satisfaction that comes from accomplishment— a solid foundation for any reader.

# Step-By-Step

The following is a simple guide to using and enjoying each of your *Illustrated Classics*™. To maximize your use of the learning activities provided, we suggest that you follow these steps:

1. *Listen!* We suggest that you listen to the read-along. (At this time, please ignore the beeps.) You will enjoy this wonderfully dramatized presentation.

2. *Pre-reading Activities.* After listening to the audio presentation, the pre-reading activities in the Activity Book prepare you for reading the story by setting the scene, introducing more difficult vocabulary words, and providing some short exercises.

3. *Reading Activities.* Now turn to the "While you are reading" portion of the Activity Book, which directs you to make a list of story-related facts. Read-along while listening to the audio presentation. (This time pay attention to the beeps, as they indicate when each page should be turned.)

4. *Post-reading Activities.* You have successfully read the story and listened to the audio presentation. Now answer the multiple-choice questions and other activities in the Activity Book.

Remember,

*"Today's readers are tomorrow's leaders."*

# Jonathan Swift

Jonathan Swift was an English author born in Dublin in 1667 of English parents. He graduated from Trinity College in Dublin and moved to England. He worked as secretary to the statesman Sir William Temple, on and off, for a period of ten years. In 1695, Swift became a minister in the Anglican Church of Ireland. After Sir Temple died, Swift became pastor to a small parish in Laracor, Ireland. He was especially concerned about the welfare and behavior of the people of his time. He wrote about the ways that the English ruled Ireland.

Swift is known for his satires on the customs and ideas of his time. He wrote *Gulliver's Travels* in 1726. It is considered a masterpiece of comic literature. Young readers enjoy *Gulliver's Travels* for the humorous make-believe world it describes. Several of the made-up words from *Gulliver's Travels,* such as "Lilliputian" and "Yahoo," have become regular words in our modern dictionaries.

Swift also wrote poetry and light verse, stories, and political articles and pamphlets.

His last 30 years were spent as the dean of St. Patrick's Cathedral in Dublin. He died in 1745 leaving his money to start a hospital for the mentally ill.

# Saddleback's *Illustrated Classics™*

# GULLIVER'S TRAVELS

## JONATHAN SWIFT

## THE MAIN CHARACTERS

Emperor of
Lilliput

Mrs.
Gulliver

King of Lamputa

Captain
Gulliver

King of Brobdingnag

It is easy for someone who travels to far away countries to tell stories to others about his adventures, but in the following story my wish is to teach and not to entertain. These are the plain facts of my experiences and I tell them because I believe that a traveler's chief goal should be to make men wiser and better.

As a young man I studied to be a doctor, taking care also to learn navigation and mathematics useful to those who intend to travel, as I always believed that sometime or other it would be my fate.

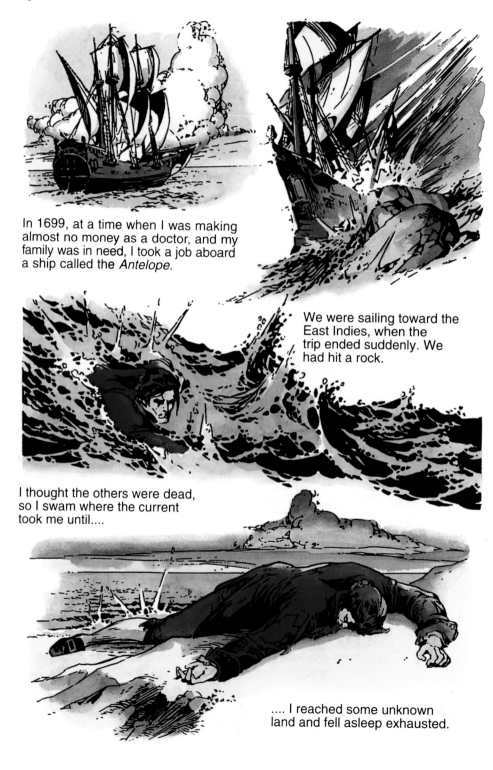

In 1699, at a time when I was making almost no money as a doctor, and my family was in need, I took a job aboard a ship called the *Antelope*.

We were sailing toward the East Indies, when the trip ended suddenly. We had hit a rock.

I thought the others were dead, so I swam where the current took me until....

.... I reached some unknown land and fell asleep exhausted.

I woke up surprised and unable to move.

I couldn't tell if I was being welcomed or not. I soon found out that I was welcome, and other surprises followed.

10

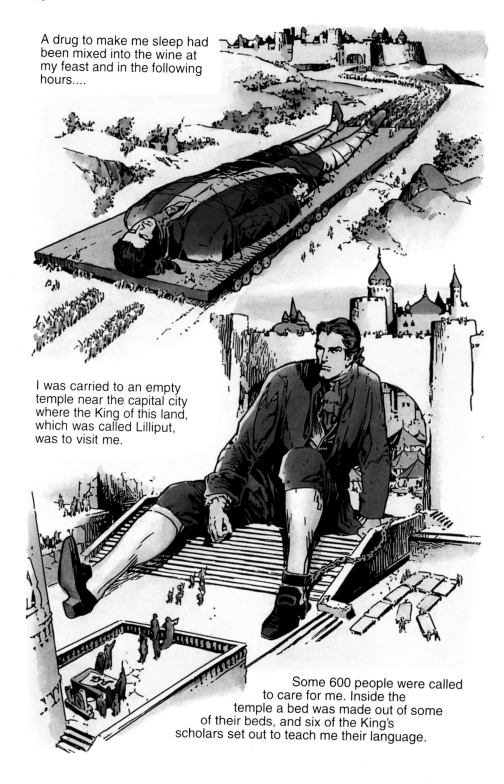

A drug to make me sleep had been mixed into the wine at my feast and in the following hours....

I was carried to an empty temple near the capital city where the King of this land, which was called Lilliput, was to visit me.

Some 600 people were called to care for me. Inside the temple a bed was made out of some of their beds, and six of the King's scholars set out to teach me their language.

As they got to know me, they let me entertain them.

Finally the day came when I said I would be loyal to the Lilliputian government, and I was given my liberty.

I was then allowed to visit the capital, Mildendo.

All the townspeople had been warned to stay off the streets.

I had never seen such beauty.

And so I came to know something of these people.

A strange disagreement divided the people of Lilliput....

.... the question of the proper end for breaking one's eggs. The legal and approved way was always from the small end. Many "Big Endians" or those who broke their eggs the other way had run to the neighboring island of Blefuscu where they were welcomed by the King of that land.

Indeed, the Blefuscian navy was just then preparing to attack Lilliput.

At the sight of me the enemy jumped from their ships and swam for shore.

My return to Lilliput was warmly welcomed, but I had unknowingly made the Admiral of the Lilliputian navy jealous.

Leaders from Blefuscu soon
arrived and signed a peace
treaty which was favorable to
Lilliput.

We dined together,
and I received an
invitation to visit
their island.

So, I asked for and was given
permission to go, not
knowing what I was getting
myself into, until some
nights later there came an
unexpected visit from a
friend.

The Admiral's jealousy of my victory at sea and the Treasurer's
cheapness over the cost of feeding me had led them to make a plan
which would have me punished.

Much to my shock, I found I had already been tried and convicted of treason, and was to be punished in three days time.

Sadly I understood that I must leave this fair land.

And so I again crossed to Blefuscu....

.... where I was again welcomed.

Three days later I made a
lucky discovery.

A small boat had been
driven close to shore by a
storm.

Then having received the King's permission and help, the more
difficult work began.

We worked together every day for a month....

Until at last all that remained was to get food and drink for my trip.

So all being ready, I sent for his Majesty's men, thanked them kindly, and set out to sea once more.

Letting the winds and weather take me where they would, in two days I spotted a ship.

I was very happy at the hope of seeing my home again.

The Captain treated me kindly and asked to hear my story. Although at first, he thought I was mad, I showed him proof which made him believe that I was telling the truth.

So I returned to my family and country and stayed for a while, earning money by telling about my adventures in Lilliput.

But liking adventure, I again took to the sea, this time aboard the *Adventurer*, headed for the Cape of Good Hope.

For a year all went well, until, we were blown off course by a storm, and came to a land, unknown to even the oldest sailor among us.

I joined a group that was going ashore for water, but hoping to find a better view, I wandered off to climb some rocks.

Suddenly, I saw the men rowing for dear life away from a great creature who stood on the shore. I ran, hoping to find some safety and a view of the country.

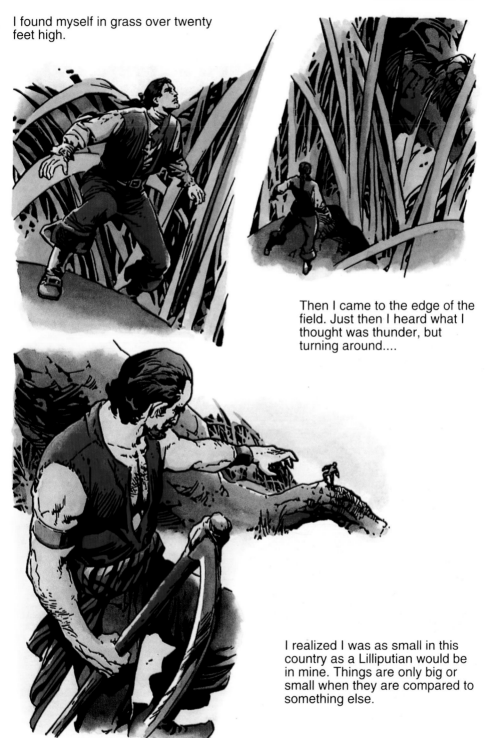

I found myself in grass over twenty feet high.

Then I came to the edge of the field. Just then I heard what I thought was thunder, but turning around....

I realized I was as small in this country as a Lilliputian would be in mine. Things are only big or small when they are compared to something else.

After looking at me for some time, the farmer who stood before me picked me up as if I were a small dangerous animal.

I spoke some words, and he seemed pleased with my voice, placed me in his pocket, and carried me to his house.

Here my travels almost ended, but I was quickly rescued and placed in the fine care of their nine-year-old daughter.

Soon she had made me seven shirts....

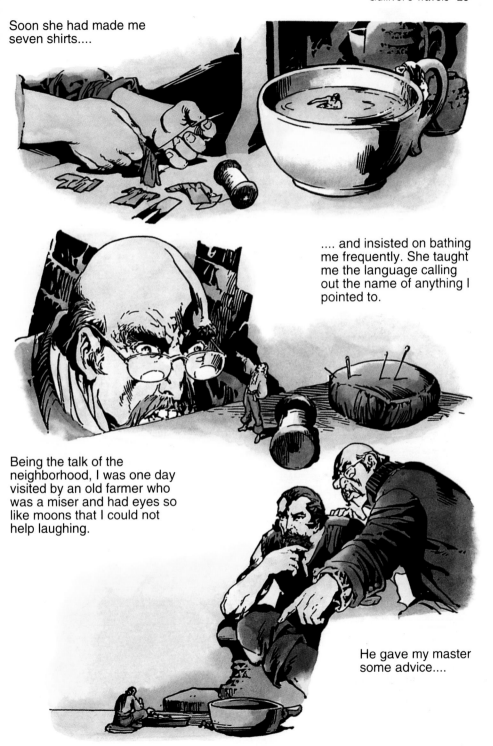

.... and insisted on bathing me frequently. She taught me the language calling out the name of anything I pointed to.

Being the talk of the neighborhood, I was one day visited by an old farmer who was a miser and had eyes so like moons that I could not help laughing.

He gave my master some advice....

The following market day I was put in a box and carried to town.

A room was hired and a man sent out to spread the news of a strange creature, me, to be seen at the Sign of the Green Eagle.

That day I was shown to twelve sets of company. I performed tricks and speeches for their amusement. My show brought so much money to the farmer that he decided to carry me on tour to bigger cities.

In the following weeks I saw much of this country, Brobdingnag. But daily horseback travel, even in the loving hands of the farmer's daughter, left me badly shaken.

Wherever we stopped, endless crowds paid to see me. I was worked for most of every day, but the more money my master got by me, the more he wanted, until, growing weaker, and weaker, I began to fear for my life.

Then, one day a messenger came and called us to Lorbrulgrud, The Pride of the Universe and their capital city, where we were to meet the Queen and her ladies.

When the great and good Queen, saw the danger I was in, and asked me if I would like to live at Court, I could not hide my joy.

I believe the farmer also had noticed my ill health and so was glad to sell me and allow his daughter to stay on as my friend and teacher.

We entered a new life in her Majesty's service at court.

The Queen brought me to the King who seemed quite surprised at my size and speech.

His majesty sent for three great scholars who looked me over quite closely but were unable to agree upon anything except that I could not have been made by regular laws of nature.

When I told the King that I came from a country with millions of people my own size, the scholars, trying to hide their ignorance, laughed, saying this must be only a story I had been taught to tell. The King, however, had a much better understanding, and believing that what I said might possibly be true, ordered that I be given a nice apartment and special care.

The queen's carpenter made me a fine box to use for bedroom and travel.

The furniture was nailed to the floor and the walls padded to prevent any accident while I was being carried.

The Queen became so fond of my company that she could not eat without me near her. Though she was considered a light eater, she took up in one mouthful as much as a dozen English farmers could eat in a meal and would nibble on a piece of meat the size of nine full grown turkeys. For a long time this was a sickening sight to me.

Sometimes I would sit with the King, who enjoyed speaking with me about the manners, religion, and government of Europe.

One evening I became quite excited while speaking about some great happening.

The King laughed and said how stupid people are to think they are so smart when even a tiny thing like me felt the same way.

Nor could I help smiling myself when I saw what I was, or had become.

But I would have lived happily in this country if my smallness had not brought certain problems.

Such as when I teased the Queen's dwarf about his size....

.... and he threw me into a silver bowl of cream. After swallowing a quart I nearly drowned and had to be put to bed.

Another time I lost my breakfast to some songbirds.

And once just made it to safety during a hail storm in the garden.

Since early times, these people, like the Chinese have had the art of printing.

I discovered that no law in that country may be longer in words than the number of letters in the alphabet, and must be written simply so all will easily understand it. Indeed, few laws are even that long.

Though I tried to make the King understand the greatness of our courts and government, his idea was that whoever could make two ears of corn, or two blades of grass to grow upon a spot of ground where only one had grown before, was of more value and glory to his country and mankind than the whole race of politicians.

I always had hoped to return home, someday, though the ship in which I arrived was the first ever known to come near that coast. Two years passed before a tour of the King and Queen to the South brought me to the only place where I might escape.

I longed to see the ocean so that, at our journey's end, although my friend was ill and could not take care of me, I begged for someone to carry me close to the shore.

Once there, he put the box down, and went off among the rocks to look for birds' eggs. Tired from the day's travel, I lay down on my bed.

Suddenly I was awakened by a great tug on the ring and hearing the noise of wings overhead, I felt myself being carried upward at great speed.

For some time the box was tossed about like a sign on a windy day. Then just as suddenly, falling....

With a terrible crash the box struck the water and, thank God, floated!

For hours I floated, each moment fearing the next would be my last, until....

I first thought I had been rescued by pygmies. And when I began to speak, the Captain asked me to please not shout.

But recalling my last rescue, I showed them certain proofs of these facts before going on with my story.

Believing me the Captain welcomed me aboard. I was delighted by everything and laughed at my own littleness as people do at their own mistakes.

When I arrived home, my daughter knelt to ask my blessing, but I was so used to looking sixty feet above me at people, I didn't even see her until she stood up....

.... and when I almost knocked my wife over trying to pick her up with one hand, she swore that I should never go to sea again. But my life would be filled with adventure again soon.

Learning of my return, the Captain of the *Hopewell* soon paid me a visit. My desire to see the world was as strong as ever, so when he offered me a good place on his next trip I could not refuse.

In the East Indies, we discovered that much of his cargo was not ready, so the Captain got us a smaller boat for trade among the islands and made me master of it.

After three days a great storm came up and blew us where it wished for five days.

Then on the tenth day pirates spotted us and easily overtook us.

I was put overboard with little food and only empty islands in sight.

Sailing from one island to the next, on the fifth day I arrived at the last and largest. I walked among the rocks not knowing what to do. The sky was perfectly clear and the sun quite hot, when suddenly I was standing in a shadow which felt more like the shade of a mountain than that of a cloud....

I saw people moving up and down and about, but I could not tell what they were doing.

Hoping to be rescued, I began waving my arms, and after a while the floating island moved closer to shore.

A voice called out to me in a language I did not understand, and a chair was lowered.

I was greeted by a strange group of people. Some of them were so deep in thought that they had to have a servant with them at all times to remind them where they are and when they should listen or speak.

In fact while I was being lead to the top of the island, they sometimes forgot what they were doing, and I was left alone.

His majesty the King took no notice of us when we came in, he was so busy thinking about some problem.

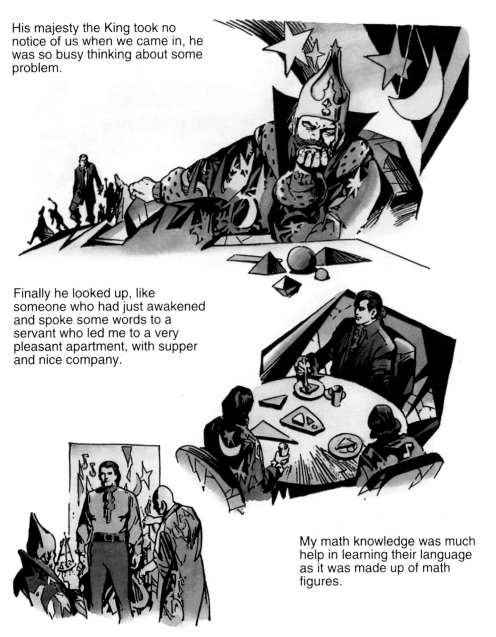

Finally he looked up, like someone who had just awakened and spoke some words to a servant who led me to a very pleasant apartment, with supper and nice company.

My math knowledge was much help in learning their language as it was made up of math figures.

The following morning I was measured for a suit of clothes in a strange way.

The suit was all uneven and did
not fit well, but I said nothing
about it and no one seemed to
notice. Indeed, there was not one
single right angle in my apartment
or anywhere on Laputa because
they disliked them.

One day I awoke to the strange music which was always
heard when the island moved. It sounded strange to my
ears, but everybody here played some instrument they
liked best.

At this moment deep in a cave,
at the heart of the island,
scientists were changing our
course, moving us East to Lagado,
the capital of the whole kingdom.

Here, with the King's
permission, I returned
to land and was sent
to visit the house of
Lord Munodi. I was
shocked by the poverty
along the way.

Though I saw many heads and hands, I could not see what they were doing, until I reached the lands of Lord Munodi which were beautiful and rich.

But with a sigh he told me that many people wanted him to tear everything down and rebuild like the rest of the country, under the direction of the Academy of Projectors. It seems that some forty years before a group from the floating island had visited Laputa and on their return, decided that they disliked everything below. So they began the Academy to be advisors over all Laputa.

Being very interested I visited the Academy which is not one building but a series of houses on both sides of a street.

Here I saw hundreds of scientists coming up with ideas which the whole country was supposed to follow, such as:

taking sunlight
from cucumbers for
use on cloudy days,
teaching spiders to weave
clothing, building houses from
the roof down, and
training pigs to do
the gardening.

However none of these ideas have been worked out completely, and in the meantime, the houses are falling down, the fields are bare, and the people are without food and clothes. I decided to try and return to England.

I hired a mule and traveled to the coast.

When I discovered that I must wait a month for a ship to England, some people I met told me to visit Glubbdubdrib, the nearby island of the Magicians.

The governor of this island had the power to call on any of the dead to serve him for twenty-four hours and so all of the work here was done by spirits.

But at the turn of a finger everyone vanished into thin air. The governor welcomed me alone and promised me I would be safe there.

When I became used to the fast comings and goings, His Highness
ordered me to call up anyone I wanted to see among all the dead
from the beginning of the world.

I learned so much. I discovered the true causes of many great events
that have surprised the world. And I also found that our history
books are often wrong.

The last person I called up was an English farmer of old. I learned how simple life used to be.

Finally the time to leave came. I visited another island on my way home, went to Japan, and at last England, a few months later.

I happily passed five months at home, but then took the job of Captain aboard the *Adventurer.* If only I had learned the lesson of knowing when I was well off.

I lost many men on the difficult trip out and was forced to pick up new sailors at Barbados.

These new men took over my ship....

.... and dropped me at the first land they saw which they swore they knew no more of than I did.

I went up into the country. The land was divided by long rows of trees, not planted but naturally growing.

Suddenly I came upon the ugliest
animal I have ever seen in all my
travels.

The monster stared at me,
surprised, but when he came closer
I hit him with the flat side of my sword. He roared
so loudly that a herd from the next field ran over.

All of a sudden they
seemed to see something
and ran off in fear.
Looking around I saw a
horse walking in the field.

When I went to pat him in thanks he gently but firmly raised his right hoof to stop me and then neighed loudly in such a way that I began to think he was speaking to someone.

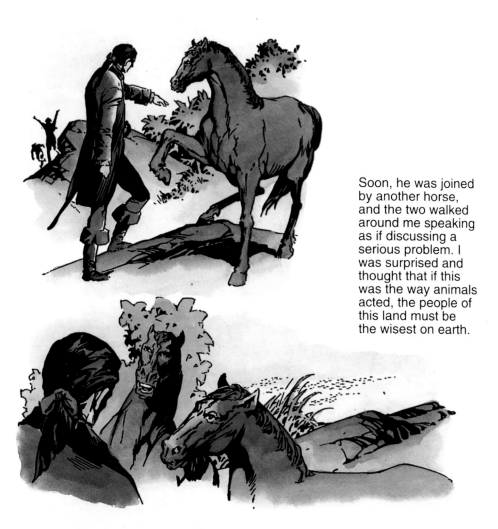

Soon, he was joined by another horse, and the two walked around me speaking as if discussing a serious problem. I was surprised and thought that if this was the way animals acted, the people of this land must be the wisest on earth.

I left the horses to speak together as they pleased, but seeing this, one neighed after me in such a way that I quickly returned to his side to see what he wanted.

After a while he led me to a
long building where he neighed
several times and was answered.

A horse came out and looked me over. He said the word "Yahoo"
several times in talking. When I repeated this word, they were
surprised and repeated it twice as if to teach me.

They led me to a cage behind
the building where I saw
three of those horrible
creatures I first met after
my landing.

My horror and surprise were
great when I saw that this
animal had the same figure as
a man.

But the horses seemed confused by my clothes since they had none.

I was offered some kind of root to eat, but refused it as politely as possible.

They then offered me some meat from the Yahoo's cage which smelled so bad that I turned away. They threw it back and it was quickly eaten.

I pointed to a cow and showed them that I should like to go and milk it.

They seemed to understand, for they led me inside and ordered a servant to open the pantry. He produced a large bowl of milk which I drank. This made me feel better.

Just then a visitor arrived to
eat dinner at the house.

He was treated with
great respect, and he
seemed interested in
me and pleased with
the way I acted. While at dinner they taught
me the words for oats, milk, fire, and water and
made me understand their worry that I had
had nothing solid to eat.

They offered me oats which I
first refused but then decided to
make a simple bread which I
toasted and ate warm with my milk.
This is not the first experiment I had made which
showed how simply a person can eat.

And never did I have an
hour's sickness while I
stayed on this island.

My main job was to learn their language, which my master and everyone in his family were happy to teach.

I was given a room away from the house but separate from the Yahoos, as these horrid man-beasts were called.

My master was most interested in hearing my story. When after many months I was at last able to explain how I had come to their land, he said I must be mistaken for I had said "the thing which was not." He could not believe it possible for Yahoos to do anything together, such as sail across the sea.

In fact, their language has no words for power, government, or punishment. That sometimes our neighbors want the things which we have was impossible in their land.

That whole countries might go to war over what color a coat or flag should be was also unbelievable to them.

And to pay someone to say a thing was untrue was worse than stupid. If speech is to make us understand one another, then saying "the thing which was not," or *lying,* makes language useless.

And finally, to my master's shock, I explained the role of horses in Europe.

The reader may wonder why I told them of our ways. I can only say that the goodness of my hosts had made me see man's actions in a different light. Indeed, after a year I decided never to return to my own kind, staying instead to watch the Yahoos in hopes of better understanding human nature....

.... and watching and learning the ways of the horses in hopes of improving myself.

Yahoos seem to be the most innocent animals, but they have a strange love for certain shining stones found in the fields of this country.

These they will dig with their hands for days... and carry away to hide....

.... always being careful that others will not discover their treasure.

Sometimes a Yahoo though young and fat, will go into a corner howling and moaning, and refuse all company.

The only way to stop this was to set him to hard work and he would always come to himself again.

The word *Houyhnhnms* in their language means a "horse" and rightly means the perfect person.

Friendship and kindness are always present among them. A stranger here from the farthest place is treated as equal to the nearest neighbor and is at home wherever he goes.

And I saw that my master showed the same love for his neighbor's children as his own.

So I settled into a life of happiness, with no doctor to destroy my body, no lawyer to ruin my fortune, and no one to watch my words and actions.

I was happier to hear my Master speak than to hear the greatest and wisest men in Europe.

And I enjoyed spending afternoons listening to him talk with his friends. They believe that when people are together, a short silence improves the conversation, and this I found to be quite true.

At first I did not feel the natural wonder which Yahoos and all other animals have for these horses, but it grew on me very quickly and with it was a love and thankfulness that they would know me from the rest of my kind.

Few events happen among a people so well united and governed by reason and love, but every fourth year on the first day of spring there was a meeting of horses from all over their nation.

Here they discussed the condition of all districts in their country. If anyone needed anything it was given to them by others who had extra.

One morning my master sadly told me that there were those who thought it was unnatural that I lived in his home and told him to send me back where I had come from. With a broken heart I prepared to leave.

And bid them good-bye.

When a passing ship came to my rescue, I begged them to leave me as I was just a poor Yahoo seeking some empty place to pass the rest of my unhappy life.

But the captain insisted that I should return to my family and country. When at last I entered the house, my wife took me in her arms and kissed me. I passed out, since I was not used to the touch of any Yahoo.

Here I take final leave of my reader and return to my simple life enjoying my own thoughts, while practicing those excellent virtues I learned among the Houyhnhnms. I will try to teach the Yahoos of my own family, and if this is possible I may in time again be able to stand the sight of humans. I at least have the friendship of two good horses with whom I speak for hours each day, and they understand me perfectly.

Captain Gulliver

THE END